I arise to meet the day,
My face is turned from
the dark of night
To gaze at the new dawn
whitening the sky.

Eskimo Song

COPYRIGHT © 1990 The Rourke Corporation, Inc.
Vero Beach, Florida 32964
Text © 1990 Terri Cowman
Illustration © 1990 Charles Reasoner

LIBRARY OF CONGRESS CATALOGING-IN-PUBLICATION DATA

Cohlene, Terri, 1950
  Ka-ha-si and the Loon / by Terri Cohlene; illustrated by Charles Reasoner.
     p. cm. — (Native American legends)
  Summary: Retells the legend of Ka-ha-si, who acquires great strength and boldness and uses them to rescue his people in times of peril. Includes information on the customs and lifestyle of the Eskimos.
  ISBN 0-86593-002-3
  1. Eskimos — Arctic regions — Legends. 2. Eskimos — Arctic regions — Social life and customs — Juvenile literature. (1. Eskimos — Legends. 2. Indians of North America — Legends. 3. Eskimos — Social life and customs. 4. Indians of North America — Social life and customs.) I. Reasoner, Charles, ill. II. Title. III. Series.
E99.E7C746 1990
398.2 089971 — dc20   AC   CIP   89-10743

Ka·ha·si
and the Loon
AN ESKIMO LEGEND

WRITTEN AND ADAPTED BY TERRI COHLENE

ILLUSTRATED BY CHARLES REASONER

DESIGNED BY VIC WARREN

Watermill Press
Mahwah, N.J.

In the land of the frozen North, there lived an Eskimo boy named Ka-ha-si. He lived with his mother in a small hunting village near the sea. Every day, all day long, Ka-ha-si slept on a warm caribou hide near the lamp in his igloo.

"Why do you not play with other children?" his mother would ask. "You should be learning how to hunt and fish so you will grow to be a good man."

But Ka-ha-si never answered. He stayed asleep by the lamp day after day, and no one could wake him.

One morning, before the sun was up, Ka-ha-si heard a faint rustling sound and felt a feather-light touch on his cheek. What is this? he thought. Who disturbs my sleep? He blinked his eyes open to see a beautiful black bird with white speckles on its back.

"Who are you?" asked Ka-ha-si.

"Hush," whispered the bird. "It is I, The Loon. I bring a message from your grandfather. Come."

Quietly, so he would not waken his mother, Ka-ha-si dressed and followed The Loon. "But I do not know my grandfather," he whispered to the bird. "He has been gone since my mother was a young girl."

"This is true," answered The Loon. "But you will meet him one day. Then he will explain."

Together, they went a great distance from the village until they came upon a flowering shrub. Ka-ha-si had never seen such a plant before. ''You must come here every day,'' said The Loon, ''and eat four leaves from this magical bush. Then you will bathe in the waters of this stream. You must be strong when your grandfather calls for you.''

Ka-ha-si did not understand, but he ate four of the bitter leaves and bathed in the icy waters. Each day after that, The Loon woke him and went with him to the magical place. Then, before he was missed, the boy would return to his warm bed by the lamp.

"He is a lazy one," people would say to Ka-ha-si's mother. "What good is he to you or to our village? He does not hunt or fish, or even help you repair your igloo."

But Ka-ha-si's mother would always answer, "He is a good son. He does not find trouble. He will learn to be a man someday, an important man, you will see."

One day followed the next until there came a season of hunger in the village. Time after time, the hunters returned empty-handed. All the animals seemed to be hiding. What were The People to do?

Ka-ha-si woke to see The Loon sitting beside him. "Why have you come, Loon?" he asked.

"Your people are starving," The Loon answered. "You must help them."

Ka-ha-si immediately went out to see what he could do. When he found the hunters gathered in the village, they all pointed and stared at him. "So you finally woke up!" someone shouted. "What is it, Lazy One, are you hungry? Do you miss the food your mother always catches for you?"

"I will help you," Ka-ha-si said.

The men laughed. "You! That is impossible. How can you do what our best hunters cannot?"

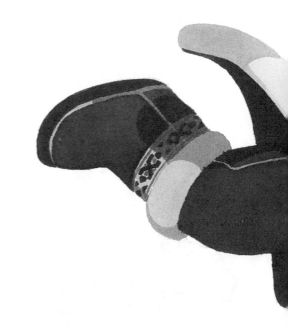

Ka-ha-si held up a big walrus skin. "Each of you take hold around this," he said. "I will stand on it, then you can throw me into the air. When I am high enough, I will be able to see where the animals are hiding."

The villagers had never before heard of such a thing, but the rumbling in their stomachs told them to try. Ka-ha-si bounced higher and higher into the air until he shouted, "There! I see a herd of walruses on an ice floe!"

Quickly, the hunters grabbed their harpoons and tied the dogs to the sledges. Ka-ha-si rode with the leader as they raced in the direction of the walruses. Soon they turned the sledges over and anchored them in the snow. Then they pushed their umiak into the water. Ka-ha-si sat silently in the bow.

"You helped us find the walruses," said a hunter, "but surely you do not think you can hunt?" Ka-ha-si said nothing.

"Let him stay," the leader said. "He may learn something."

They paddled through rough waters to the ice floe. Each time they drew near enough to throw a harpoon, a giant wave pushed them back, and the weapon missed its mark. Finally, the men were exhausted and they decided to turn back.

Ka-ha-si stood up. "Paddle close once more," he said. "I know what to do." The hunters murmured in disbelief, but did as he asked. When they drew close, a powerful wave lifted the umiak high into the air, and Ka-ha-si jumped from the boat onto the ice floe.

Before the startled walruses had time to attack or dive into the sea, the boy began knocking their heads together. Then he picked up the stunned animals and hurled them one by one into the waiting umiak. When it could hold no more, Ka-ha-si jumped back into the boat.

The hunters couldn't believe what happened. It took many men to drag a walrus. How could a boy do such a thing as this? When they returned to their village, there was much rejoicing. The People wanted to thank Ka-ha-si, but he was nowhere to be seen. His mother finally found him, curled up, asleep by the lamp.

Days passed and Ka-ha-si still slept by the fire, waking only to go secretly with The Loon each morning to their special place. The people soon forgot how he had saved them from hunger. They remembered only his laziness.

One day, strangers came to the village, bringing with them a fierce giant. "Who among you can defeat our champion?" called one of the strangers. "Or are you all too weak?"

The giant was twice the size of the strongest man in the village, but it would cast shame on their people to refuse such a challenge. There was nothing else to be done. One by one, the men took their turn to fight.

a-ha-si woke to see The Loon sitting beside him in the sunlight. "Why have you come, Loon?" he asked.

"Your people are threatened by a fierce giant," The Loon said. "You must help them."

Ka-ha-si immediately went out to see what the trouble was. He reached the circle of shouting people, just as the giant tossed the last hunter aside like a mosquito. Laughing, the giant shouted, "You fight like women! Is there no one among you who can fight like a man?"

Ka-ha-si stepped forward. "You have not yet challenged me!"

The giant looked down. "Ha! Now you send a boy to fight? I will throw him away like an old bone!" With that, he reached out and grabbed Ka-ha-si's arms, but he could not move him. The giant tried again and again, but it was as though Ka-ha-si were anchored to the ground.

Then the boy reached out and with one hand picked the giant up and tossed him beyond the last igloo in the village. The People cheered, and the strangers hurried to carry their champion off in shame. The People tried to thank their hero, but he was gone. Again, his mother found him, asleep in his favorite place by the lamp.

Soon afterward, harder times yet fell on The People. With great shaking of the earth, the mountains began moving toward the sea. Closer and closer they came until they reached the edge of the village. "Ka-ha-si!" The People shouted. "Wake up, wake up! You must save us!"

But Ka-ha-si slept on, and The People took anything they could carry and pulled their umiaks and kayaks to the shore. Just then, The Loon swooped over their heads to Ka-ha-si's igloo.

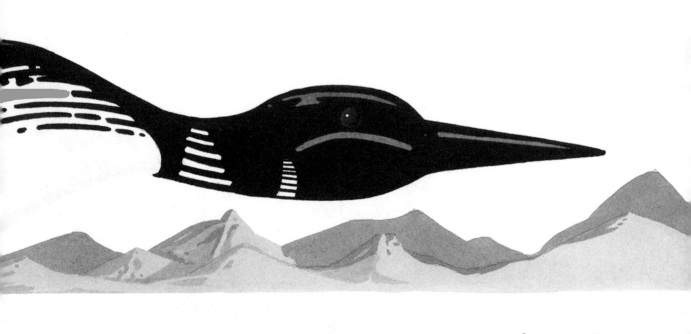

a-ha-si awoke to feel the Earth's trembling. "What is this, Loon?" he asked.

"It is the mountains," answered The Loon. "They are attacking your people. You must help."

When Ka-ha-si crawled out of his igloo, the villagers were pushing their boats into the water. "Wait!" called the boy. "I will stop this terrible thing." With that, he hurried past all the igloos that now lined the shore. He held up his hands shouting, "Go back! Go back where you belong, my grandfather would have it so!"

But the mountains continued their march to the sea. "Come, Ka-ha-si! Save yourself," The People called.

Ka-ha-si ignored them and laid his hands against the biggest mountain. With all his strength, he pushed harder and harder until finally it was back where it belonged. Then he pushed another mountain, and another, until they were all in their places.

After this, he took a giant piece of driftwood from the beach and dredged a space between the mountains and the village all the way to the sea. This became a river, which the mountains could never cross.

As The People sang with joy, The Loon came to Ka-ha-si and said, "You have done well. Your grandfather, He-Who-Holds-Up-The-Earth, needs you. He is old and becomes weak. He bids you hurry."

Unseen by the villagers, Ka-ha-si got into his kayak and paddled after The Loon. When they were far from shore, a giant whirlpool caught the small boat, swirling it fiercely. With all his strength, Ka-ha-si could not free himself.

"Do not worry," calmed The Loon. "It is but the way to your grandfather." At last, Ka-ha-si understood. He dropped his paddle, and allowed the sea to swallow him up.

When The People searched for Ka-ha-si, he was nowhere to be seen. His mother looked for him by the fire, but he was not there. "Where is my son?" she called. But before anyone could answer, The Loon landed beside her.

"Do not worry," he said. "Ka-ha-si is safe. He has gone to be with his grandfather."

As The Loon explained, the villagers understood how important Ka-ha-si really was. In all the days that followed, The People sang of his deeds. And each time they felt the Earth tremble, they knew it was only Ka-ha-si, The Strong One, shifting the Earth from one shoulder to the other.

THE ESKIMO

CHUKCHI   *Chukchi Sea*

Bering Sea

NORTH ALASKAN

Arctic Ocean

Beaufort Sea

BERING SEA

ALASKA

KUTCHIN

KHOTANA

ALEUTIAN

YUPIK

MACKENZIE

HARE

Gulf of Alaska

CANADA

ARCTIC CIRCLE

KASKA

DOGRIB

YELLOW KNIFE

ESKIMO HOMELAND

The Eskimos populated the coast of Greenland and the northern-most regions of Asia and North America. Scientists think they walked across the Bering Sea to North America on a land bridge that has long since been covered by the ocean.

An Eskimo family from the Hudson Bay region wears beautifully decorated fur clothing.

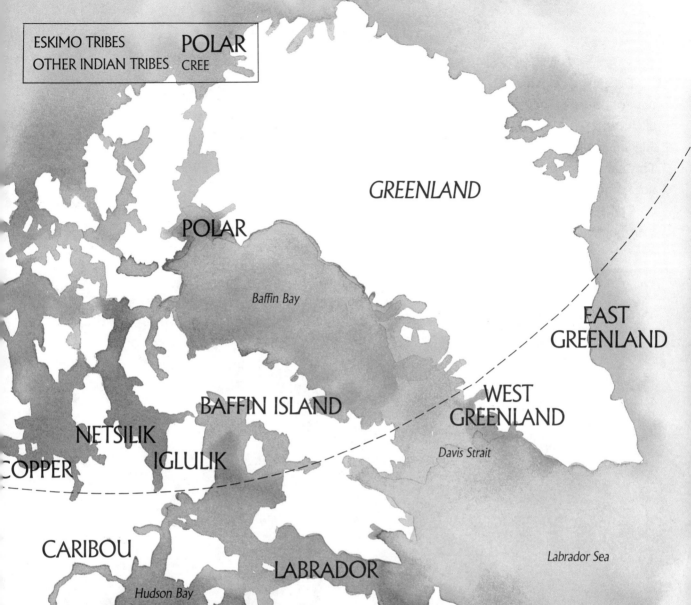

ESKIMO TRIBES **POLAR**
OTHER INDIAN TRIBES CREE

GREENLAND

POLAR

Baffin Bay

EAST
GREENLAND

BAFFIN ISLAND

WEST
GREENLAND

NETSILIK

Davis Strait

COPPER IGLULIK

CARIBOU

Labrador Sea

LABRADOR

Hudson Bay

The extreme Arctic climate makes it one of the most difficult places in the world to live. Temperatures range from as cold as minus 50 degrees Fahrenheit to a few warm summer days of 70 degrees. Since there's very little rain or snow, Eskimos get their drinking water from sea ice, which loses its saltiness after it's over a year old.

In the Arctic, the sun stays low to the horizon, if it rises at all. Depending on the distance to the North Pole, the night can last several months. Likewise, there can be several months of daylight in the spring and summer. Very few plants can grow under these conditions. Since the only wood they ever saw was driftwood, many people thought trees grew at the bottom of the sea.

35

ESKIMO PEOPLE

Depending on where they live, Arctic natives may call themselves Yupik, Iglulik or Inuit, which all mean "The People." "Eskimo" is from an Algonquian word meaning "eaters of raw meat." This name was given to them by outsiders, and is not normally used among their own clans.

The People worked hard just to survive. The men hunted, fished, made tools and built igloos,

Ice fishing—an important source of food during the spring.

sledges and boats. The women cleaned the fish and game, treated hides and made clothing. They prepared food and cared for the houses, children and dogs. The children learned the skills they would need as adults.

Besides survival difficulties, the extreme weather had other important effects on the Eskimos' lives. For example, they had no measure of time. Without watches or the sun or moon to guide them, they could only rely on how they felt. If they were tired, they slept. If they were energetic, they went about their work.

The cold and dark also affected their emotional health. To keep from becoming too cranky or moody, The People liked to laugh and joke. They played string games, ball games and sports. Many winter evenings passed with songs, dances and storytelling.

The drums this North Alaskan Eskimo orchestra used were made from whale stomachs stretched over wooden frames.

Although sealskin was popular for making Eskimo clothing, fur from other animals was also used. This parka is sewn from caribou, reindeer, and mountain sheep fur, with marten and wolf fur trim. The boots are made of white wolf, dog and reindeer fur.

Snow-block igloos were built by the Eskimo for winter shelter in the ▷ far north. While most igloos housed only five or six people, this igloo, photographed in 1903, was 27½ feet across and stood 12½ feet high. Furs covered sleeping platforms, and kettles hung over oil lamps.

FOOD, CLOTHING AND SHELTER

Eskimos relied almost completely on the sea. They netted fish or hunted seal, walrus, sea lion and whale. In the summer, they traveled south to fish for salmon, hunt caribou, and pick berries. They often ate their food uncooked.

Besides food, animals provided oil for lamps or lotions, and furs and skins for clothing, blankets and shelter. Women tanned the hides and spent hours each day sewing mukluks, parkas and snow pants using sinew thread. In the winter, everyone wore two sets of clothing. First, they put on a set with the fur side in, then a set with the fur side out. This kept them warm and dry even in the coldest temperatures.

During warmer weather, The People usually lived inland in igloos of skin, wood, mud, or sod. Ice igloos, or "igluvigaqs," were built for hunting and fishing near the winter sea. They could be constructed in less than an hour when hunters were caught in a storm far from home. Igloos were simply furnished with a central drying rack and beds padded with dried leather. An oil lamp made of soapstone provided light and warmth.

Yupik Eskimos of western Alaska believed that a spirit named Tunghak controlled all the animals. This mask was used in dances to please Tunghak, so that fishing and hunting would be good.

ESKIMOS TODAY

Many of the Arctic's native people live there still. They do not have reservations as do many Native Americans farther south, but the government has allotted certain land to them individually and as villages.

Few live strictly as they did in the past. They now use snowmobiles more than dogsleds, and their umiaks are equipped with motors. Men and women may have jobs with oil companies or have careers as doctors, lawyers or teachers.

Eskimos remember their proud history with art and music. Winter evenings still find laughing Arctic people dancing and telling stories in the village singing house.

Petroglyphs are paintings on rocks. Even though very old, these drawings of whales and animals are so simple they seem modern.

These twin Eskimo girls modeled their fur parkas for a photographer in 1905.

IMPORTANT DATES

1001	Greenland colonized by Icelander, Erik the Red	1880	Beginning of Alaska Gold Rush
1492	Columbus reaches North America	1909	Robert Peary discovers the North Pole
1728	Vitus Bering surveys Bering Sea for Russia	1924	Native Americans born in U.S. declared citizens.
1799	Charter of Russian-American Company, which ran fur monopoly in what is now Sitka, Alaska	1942-48	1,523 miles of Alcan Highway built from Dawson Creek, B.C., to Fairbanks, Alaska, at a cost of $138,000
1867	U.S. purchases Alaska from Russia for $7,200,000	1967	Alaska Federation of Natives formed
		1968	Oil discovered off Alaska's north shore

An Eskimo family could move all its belongings with a large dogsled like this.

Figures like this walrus-man show the importance Eskimos gave the animals they hunted.

Eskimo artists used bow-drills to carve beautiful designs in ivory, wood and bone.

43

An Eskimo hunter gets ready for a seal hunt in his kayak.

GLOSSARY

Caribou: Arctic reindeer of North America.

Eskimo: Algonquian Indian word for the Arctic people meaning "eaters of raw meat."

Floe: Large sheet of ice floating in the sea.

Harpoon: Barbed spear for hunting large fish or sea mammals.

Igloo: Arctic house, whether made of hides, wood, sod, or ice.

Kayak: Sealskin boat for one person, with covering to tie around the waist.

Mukluk: Footwear.

Special headgear was worn to please the spirits of the animals the Eskimos hunted.

Sinew: Animal tendon used for making ropes or thread.

Sledge: Arctic sled.

Umiak: Large, open boat that can carry over a ton.

45